Butterflies Turned Bitter

Caroline Prater
Copyright © 2024 Caroline Prater
All rights reserved.

To the ones who've shown me the meaning of unconditional love -

I'm honored to have your influence in my life.

I'm a better person because of you.

Thank you for allowing me the space to heal, and reminding me of the highest standards for how my heart should be treated.

Thank you,
thank you,
thank you.

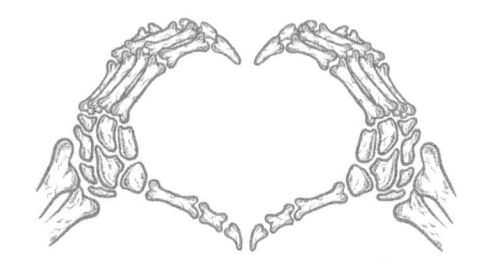

THE FALLING

I never said I would be an easy kind of love

I am
a stand underneath your balcony
and scream your name,
an intense
kind of love

I am
a hand beneath your shirt
as we drive down the road,
a light your soul on fire,
kind of love

I am not a quiet
or an easily satisfied,
kind of love

I am
a bite your shoulder
and pull your hair,
a blurred lipstick and bruises,
kind of love

I am
a ragged breath
that settles deep into your lungs,
a run my fingers
over your darkest parts
and not run,
kind of love

I'm an "I would gladly drink the poison
just to die with you,"
a star-crossed lovers,
kind of love

My love will wrap around you recklessly,
an unforgettable,
kind of love

And remember, I never said
I would be a quiet,
kind of love

I have never known how to be that easy,
peaceful,
kind of love

Coffee rings left on the windowsill
an aftertaste of love
accidentally spilled

You run your fingers down my spine
somewhere in the night
I made you mine

On this chilly fall morning
in this bed with you
my heart shouts no warning

It does not run away
as if being chased

No, it beats slow and steady
under the heat of your gaze

I am a slow-burning lover
like the lingering embers in your fire's ash
the lightning you envy may strike hot
but it's not built to last

I want to make love slowly
in a hammock
with the kiss of a breeze
I want to be able to
fold into your arms with ease

I want our passion to warm you
deep in your veins
and when I say I love you
I need you to know
I will stay

If you would take a chance on what's broken

You'll see how beautiful life can be
looking through shattered glass

Shimmering rays of light
reflecting on a still-broken heart

praying you don't see someone's discarded toy

but a breathing work of art

Dear future lover,

please hold me steady when I waiver

hold my secrets without judgment

roam every inch of me

love every version

even the ones I'm not proud of

especially the ones I'm not proud of

To love someone new
doesn't mean the old one
shouldn't still exist inside of you

Our hearts are all filled
with locked rooms
where past lovers haunt

Each love is just different
each one a unique imprint
on a wayward heart

I feel peace from your touch
where I once only felt fear
if only you could see the light
you emit when you're near

You're forever my favorite sunset

A blank page sits in front of me
and all I read is your name

I crave a steady hand
and a patient touch
someone who understands
what it's like when the world
becomes too much

A light
when the darkness feels
like it will swallow me up

What if there was a world with no one but us?

Would you give in to that lost boy and have fun with me?
Healing all of his parts that have been hurt?

Would you give in to that lost girl and feel love with me?
Could you be the one I give my heart to on this earth?

Your words wrapped around me
like a melody
sweet, did your notes feel against my skin

You don't even know me yet
you think since you've been inside my body,
you've seen inside my head?

You don't know that small animals bring me to tears
or how I felt adrift for so many years
or that I love fresh flowers in my home
their blooms remind me of my lost hope

You don't know that I lost a child,
while I was a child
or that I watched my parents argue
for most of my life
or that my needs
have been met with inconsistency
from the second I was born
a heart forged from the hot and cold
but begs to be warmed

You don't know me yet

The dimple on your cheek
you cant see
that comes out
when you speak

of all the little things
that makes your heart expand

like the night when
I watched you
watch your favorite band

Your neck was sweaty
and your hair a mess
in that moment,
I could not love you any less

Drive my mind mad
keep my heart safe
and I am yours forever

Lead me in nightly worship
caress me with your holy touch
infinite possibilities lie before us
let's find glory in each other
before the world becomes too much

You threw me over your shoulder
screaming, laughing, crashing
we jumped into the water

Submerged for just a second
you pulled me closer in the current
never felt more in love
than what was exploding
in my chest at that moment

I miss the feeling
of being best friends with you
with love swimming all around us
in that sparkling pool

Fireflies are my favorite thing about June

I feel a shift in the air when I see them light up the evening
a lightness floats in on the summer breeze

the days get longer

the smells get sweeter

time slows down

I sit on my porch
and let the sounds of the city pour into place
I hear neighborhood noises and community chatter
I see the planes returning home and carrying those seeking adventure elsewhere
I feel the sun kiss my skin

Most nights
I wish the fireflies
would pick me up and take me
to the home where they find their magic
to the source that lights up the darkest of nights
and as I watch them dance across this evening dusk

I close my eyes and remember the feeling
of having you in my arms
and I wonder if the home I seek to find in them
I may still
one day
find with you

You'll be my rock
and I'll be your river
while you steady my roar
in your touch I will quiver

I'll mold your insides
your edges I'll tame
swept up in love's current
until I take your last name

Little things, magnets.

Like the one you brought home from your trip.

Whoever thought to capture a city
with tacky lettering and paint that's sure to chip?

The smile on your face
when you handed it to me,
proud of the treasure you found.

I just couldn't quite believe
with all the things you might see,
you looked around
the city with new eyes,

and found something
that made you think of me.

He stayed the night
he woke with me
and when the sunlight streamed in

He pulled me into him
like an extension of limbs
he'd been missing his whole life

Remember that night
we lay under the stars
you were my blanket
I fell asleep in your arms

Nose to nose
skin on skin
that was the moment
I let you in

And as we watched
the heavens paint the sky
I took a deep breath
and looked in your eyes

My breath caught
when the love in yours
mirrored my own

I knew then
I had found
my home

THE TRYING

I am scared that the distance will bring
only time zones
and moments caught in between

Trying hard to make things last
but it feels like our time together
will come to pass

When "Hey honey, how was your day?"
turns into, "I'm sorry, I can't talk right now
I'm going to be late"

So we rush off the phone
and I sit all alone
wishing for just another second
of your dial tone

Each time we speak
I feel the distance between us start to creep
into our hearts and into our way
pretty soon
we'll run out of words we can say

You'll go your way
and I'll go mine
I hope that one day we'll run into each other
and remember how we once made each other smile
god, I haven't felt that way in a while

Then maybe we'll finally see
the biggest heartbreak isn't distance
but all the things we would never be

Maybe you do feel the weight of my unanswered questions

Will you snap at me in anger over something I have no sanction?

Is it all an act?
When I wake up tomorrow will all of your bags be packed?

Are you worth the sacrifice of my body to bear our children?
Will you support me through the most vulnerable time,
     when my life won't be just mine?

Will you laugh with me over silly things?
Will you share inside jokes and secret memories?

Will you heal with me so our babies hearts
won't feel as heavy as mine does today?

And I can't say I'm sorry for this weight,

but I hope it does get easier to carry before it's too late

White sheets draped over your shoulder
the morning sun comes in
we're both another day older
but never any wiser

The sweetness of the sunrise
is tainted by the weight of our words
thrown at each other last night

The invisible wounds left in the open
if you saw the marks left on my soul
would you love them?

I think I need you to love them

I only wanted to wear
your shirt to bed
and have a safe space
to rest my head

A tiny space just for me
somewhere in your life
I don't think, ever once
I gave you the ultimatum
to make me your **wife**

Pretty words can bend your
will and shape the sea
but they will never be
the arms I crave around me

Pretty words won't hold me at night
and your pretty words will never make it all right
what letters can you throw together
that will give me yet another reason to stay?

I, and love, and you

Say them enough
I'll let myself believe they are true

A string of words so pretty
you could write a song
when it was only the honest ones
I needed from you
all along

Maybe I liked hearing you say
you would bloody your hands for me

Something about
the fierceness in those words
and the fire in your kiss
demanded more than my heart was used to

For it had never known a protective love
but how quickly that can turn
into a possessive love
and my heart
never knew the difference

I need you to know
that we meant something

I need you to know
that you were never a waste of time

I would go back and do it all again
just to recross every line

The love in your eyes
lingered within a veil of possession

And there I was
looking at you,
looking at everyone else,
look at me

But did you ever once
really see?

Your eyes memorized every inch
of my body,
but missed my soul

Can I will the longing from my mind to yours?

Will I ever find
someone with the patience
to let me be free?

When you hold me on the bad days
as they inevitably will come
the tears will fall
my chest will ache
where did this enemy come from?

And I will fight every urge
to give into that slow, comforting bleed
as I try to exhale the weight of my past
I beg that you help me
should I stumble to my knees

So if the bad days come
as they inevitably will
when the furrow in my brow seems permanent
and the locks on my heart bring forth a chill

I hope you remember the night
you held me under the moon
and the warmth from my lover's touch

Please remember, I will always rise again
even if on my bad days,
the world seems a little too much

Temper flares and bedroom stares
what a toxic muse you are
to put your hands on me
then beg for forgiveness

You already know this
but I'm writing to say
you made me feel *insignificant*

And after burying
yourself inside me for a year
I never even saw where you lived

I just wanted to know
about your morning routine
and what my smell would be like
on your sheets

I don't want to compete with a ghost
when I'm here
ready and willing to love you

Maybe it's a primordial need
to hear you say, "you're all mine"
our time on earth
is too precious to be wasted
will you ever be ready
to recross that line?

I know you'll never burn for me
the way I burn for you
I'll leave scorch marks on your skin
and you'll paint my heart
the prettiest of blues

We'll play pretend
I'll act like I don't know
where you've been
you'll act like no one else
has been kissing my lips
and we'll fall
into each others arms again

I'll be your devil tonight

I'll slip my halo off
and set my wings aside

I'll happily be
the villain in your eyes

Can you taste how it would feel
to let me in?

I'll glady be your favorite sin

"Of course"

What I should have said
as I sat across from you
and asked the questions
heavy beating in my head

"It changes everything"

When you said you didn't know
as we were growing close
if someone were to call you up
you'd crawl back home

We were lightning strikes
lost in our storms
more combustible
then the fireworks show
we caught a glimpse
of in the sky
wrapped in your arms
and a pink sunset dusk
a humid 4th of July

We were the sparks
lasting through a cold night
in late December
the kind of burn
that could last a life time
but there can't be only one
who is willing to stoke the fire

My heart has been broken
by hands who weren't yours

But I'd carry each piece
across an ocean of blue
to get them to you

So will you open your hands
and help me carry the weight?

Or do my jagged edges
remind you of your mother's dinner plate
you saw smashed on the floor
as you stared
frozen at the door

Could you ever think of me
as something
that wouldn't make
you bleed?

Should I give my love to you
who only views it as a burden?

For my love is not such a heavyweight
for those ready to hold it

It seems you never dared
to ask the questions
that would lead
to the depths of my heart

To know all the things
you wondered about me
where would we even start?

So instead we'll lay
in a comfortable silence
my head on your chest
wrapped in each other's arms
strangers turned lovers,
never friends
both of us too terrified
to find out how we'd end

Slice me with words you know will cut the deepest
when I pull too hard on the strings
you like to wrap around my wrists

I should have known
from the moment I let you in

Your love was the kind
that would leave marks on my skin

WHAT DO YOU WANT FROM ME?

It's been 8 months now
and I'm not sure how I can be
more perfect or PRISTINE

Tell me, please
WHAT DO YOU WANT FROM ME?

On the days when I needed your love
a little longer
you said that I'd be better
if only I could be
a little stronger

But I am tired
of the strength that's been
etched into my bones
a litany of pain
with nowhere else to go

And so I'll settle for this love
because it's all I've ever known

I should've said lean on me
I should've carved our names into a tree
Marked in the wood we stood beneath
Our little moment
Of eternity

THE ENDING

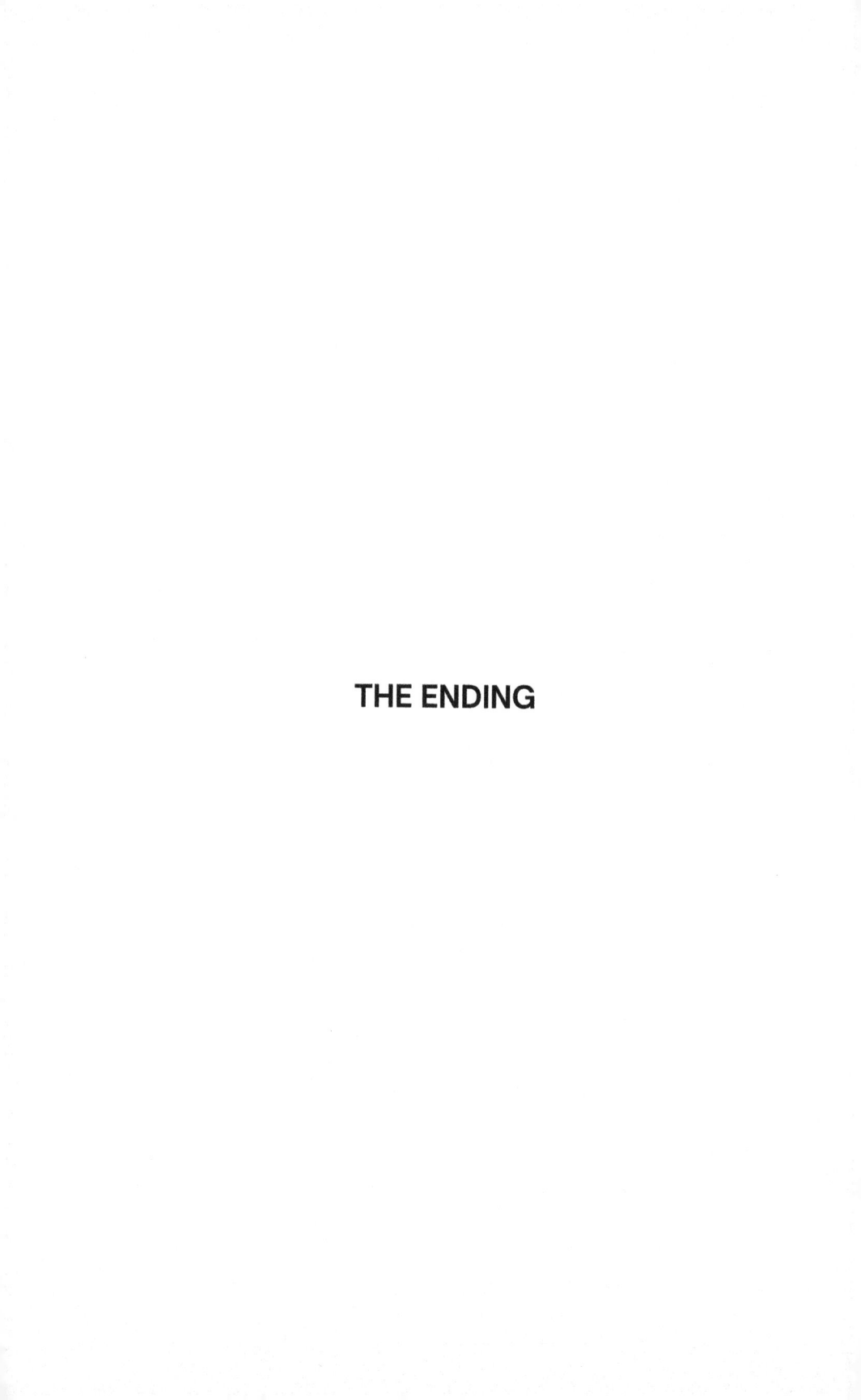

Did you get what you wanted?
When you found your way to the ends of the earth
was your mind still haunted?

Did the ghosts of your heart
still sing you to sleep?
And tell me when you dreamed,
was it ever of me?

It's a subtle change
the change in your smile
each time your heart breaks

Excuses drip off the tip of your tongue
your words are laced
with all the damage that you've done

I hope you wake up
before you find yourself
suffocated
by all the fires
you'll never outrun

I heard about the secrets
spilled in the back of the tour bus
could've won an Oscar
for your performance

Loved to push
until I bent
only ever a game to you
a pretty puppet to play with
in your life of pretend

We don't have to talk
but would you come over?
I'll let my hands tell you
I'm seventy days older.

We don't have to talk
but would you hold me?
Your lips can tell me of your travels
and I'll find peace in your heartbeat.

We don't have to talk
but would you let me love you?
Just for one more night
and we can try again
when the morning is new.

You never once asked to
take a picture together
but I was too proud to ask
for what I need

Seemed like your eyes
always longed for subjects
I could never be

You buried yourself inside my heart
But to the occasion, you could not rise

Let's walk down this dead-end road
and paint pretty pictures
of all the places we'd like to go

Like that trip to the coast to see your father
and how we sat at sunset by the water

When the pieces of you
began to fall for the pieces of me
we laid it all bare
down by the sea

With cautious hands and lingering lips
you held my heart between your fingertips
you traced the cracks
from where it'd first been broken
as you held my gaze
with a promise unspoken

Take my hand down this dead-end road
where we promised we'd never be
like the ones who lived here before

We'd build a home
where our souls could settle
and seal a new life intertwined
with rings of precious metal

With happy hands and healing hearts
it seemed that after all life threw at us,
we'd finally get a fresh start

But the past always had a way
of knocking on your door
and all those pretty pictures
wound up on the floor

When insecurities
led to begging for forgiveness
down on bended knees

It's hard to hear the words
when you aren't listening
to my voice that now shakes
and a heart that's been crippling

Over promises that turned out broken
from all the words we chose
to leave unspoken

Sometimes I wish I could go back
to that day by the water
if I knew then what I know now
I'd hold you even longer

A time when we imagined
all the places we would go
but it's time we go our separate ways
down this dead-end road

And I hope you never forget,
that you once
held a flower in your hand
and willingly
watched her wilt

I don't want scraps of time
I want *everlasting*

I don't want pieces of your heart
I need its *entirety*

I don't want you just for now
I wanted us *forever*

The night you said you couldn't find
love for me anymore
I found myself scattered to pieces
on a friends bathroom floor

A sentence said so carelessly
so you could feel relief and be rid of me
as tears slid down my cheek so quietly
and your words sank
into my anatomy

The night you said that love
had never been our reality
And I felt something
die inside of me

One day
you will stop loving him

Your mind will wander to him less often
memories won't replay in your mind
every time you close your eyes

With time also comes perspective
and a deep understanding of why

It will get better
there is a version of you
who knows this to be true

I'll be the bad guy
I'll take the blame
I'll carry the weight of the hate
you place on my name

I'll be the villain
I walked out the door
too many chances given
broke me to my core

I'll be the slut
I'll take the blame
should I feel guilty
at the way he says my name?

I'll be the bad guy
I left you alone
you sat and smiled
as you turned my heart to stone

I told you what I needed

laid out a map for how to love me

*and you still
couldn't find the time to read it*

We're just friends
said over again
repeated until
it was our end

A painted on Barbie
you talked shit about
and little ole me
didnt scream or shout

It's not her fault
we could've been friends
but you didn't care
to let me in

Or maybe it is
and she's your original string
if she waits around long enough
maybe you'll finally be free
to fall into her arms
when there is nothing left of me

I try to pretend like it didn't hurt
now that I know the road we were on together
led you back to her

You retraced the steps of an old lover
I once told you about so long ago
like I drew the map
for you to rip open my scars
but how was I to know?

Still can't take accountability for your actions
at the ripe old age of 34
so you ran back to somewhere
that would never ask for more

Of the version of a man who couldn't reach
the places he was begged to find
in order to build those dreams
we talked about
so late at night

But if there is one thing I've learned
on this road, I often travel alone

It's that re-reading chapters won't change the past
and if you find yourself in an old lover's arms
the ego high you're jonesing for will never last

Pour another glass
with your trembling hands
the consequence of your actions
led her into the arms
of another man

Your eyes gulp her in
as she floats across the room
tangled games of love
ended much too soon

Your fingers itch
for the memory
of how they felt
on her skin

A lit flame
under your touch
if only your head
had leaned into the rush

I tried to show you my heart.
but how can you see me through blind eyes
and a clenched jaw?

Resisting us for what?
To prove you're so tough?

To prove how much you loved someone else?
You are willing to lose me
because what you feel is too much?

Or maybe that's just what I tell myself
on the mornings when I shower off your touch

I knew it from the night we met
at the top of the stairs
when a sunrise met a sunset

Two souls tied together
in one silhouette

Dancing around the hurt
tripping over our past
two broken hearts
couldn't find a way to work

Tried to find every reason under our sun
to convince myself I was loved by you

God, I got so lost in your eyes
but next time

I'll know to run

You took all the love I gave
just to turn around and bury my heart
within your string of shallow graves

I couldn't leave you
so I had to burn
every touch
every smile
every memory
word by word

I cleansed us
regret by regret
and finally let you go
as the sun set

I hadn't the courage
to say them to your face
so the flames will learn our secrets
as scattered new beginnings fall into place

You'll never hear the fuel
that kept this fire alive
a love story buried
in the ashes

A cleansing
on the darkest of nights

Was I always a pawn in your game?
Another warm body with a different name?

Filled my heart with dreams
that would never come true

All so your ego would feel important
because finally

somebody
loved
you

You recycle the same words to the same girls
and still think the world views you as unique?
As if, the trail of lies you left behind
would magically open the world at your feet

But that's not how the real world works
and I pray you find out soon
before another girl stumbles on your love
and you play her like a fool

Dead roses dance on the wall
a shadow
a flicker
a flame

a heart
with no where left to fall

I watched my words sink into you
like a handprint on your cheek

At the loss of a girl
who tried so hard to set you free

The lingering sting
of your cold new reality

I hate knowing that
you touched my skin
that I let you in
all your misplaced love
found its way to me
then her again

Take back your kisses
and your dreams
always looking for more
than what I could give,
it seems

Take it all back
there's never any fun to be had
when you fake a love like that

Tears stained my cheeks
more than blush ever did

And maybe I imagined
all of the light
you brought into my life

Because I needed so desperately
to see in the dark

When she takes the midnight rose
it will sting the fingertips
that itched to feel it so

A surface level tear
the same color as the painted sorrow
on her blood stained lips

There's a storm rolling in
and the rain begins to drench her senses
melding with the rivers
already flowing down her face
she's ready to drown In a wave of memories
she just can't seem to erase

Alone in a garden filled with stone,
there stands a broken hearted silhouette
dancing with the phantom
she still carries in her chest

The thunder is their band
and they will spin round,
and round
limb lost in limb
his skeleton holds her heart in his hands
this phantom love will never know
what it truly means to grow old
what she'd give for one more last dance

The rain begs to take the heartbroken lovers away
her phantom lover will hold her close
a whisper in her ear
her favorite ghost

She lifts her head for one more haunted kiss
placed upon her blood-stained lips
one final memory she couldn't resist

Her midnight rose
now covered in stone
their love will live on
if only deep in her bones

You were too busy making notes
of everything we weren't
to ever appreciate all the things we were

All of the ways we didn't feel like the past
Everything we could've been,
if we'd had the courage to make it last

No matter where you go in this world
No matter who you touch with your light
I will always be happy you touched my heart
Even if it hurts tonight

You fall out of love with me
when I'm not in your view

But the moon leaves you for days
and your heart sighs in relief

When you see her glow anew

To deny that I love you
is to deny the part of me
that breathes

To tell myself this isn't
heartbreak, would mean
erasing the night we danced
beneath the trees

When the moon bore witness
to the things
we wanted to be

It's because of her I know we were real

No matter how far you run
to save yourself from the
things you refuse to feel

The sky is pink
But I feel blue
So I sit on our bench
And remember a time
I once held you

I saw our little life
I saw our little kids
How sweet you'd be
When they came rushing in
From playing too hard
In our little yard
All those basic channels
Got us pretty far

I wanted to share my light
And my dark nights
All of the good and bad
At the end of the day
I wanted to be your best friend

I don't want to be looked at
Like a problem to fix
Or rejoiced for
How well I can take a hit

I wanted you to love me through it all
But I for one, know that order is tall

I hope I wake from this dream soon
Where you knock on my door
Take me on the floor
And finally admit, *"I was always yours"*

It was the type of love that used you all up
the kind you may recover from
but you'd never be the same again
once the scar tissue sets in

I can never tell my friends
you didn't love me honestly

Because you told me over and over
you'd never love me the way I need

I have one of the warmest souls I know,
but you've made me remember
it's easier to exist when it's cold

And I do not possess
enough broken pieces
to fill up the holes
you refuse to close
in your heart

but I think I knew that
from the start

You say to me
"have more compassion,
more tact,"
when is a good time
to inconvenience you with my feelings?

Even your grief
is not an excuse
to treat me like that

You've told me repeatedly
that you could never be
the man for me

So why
didn't I take you at your word,
and leave?

I will not let the thoughts of loss overtake me
for I have gained so much
by losing you

But I remember
how you looked at me
go on, tell me another lie
and say we didnt mean anything

When I was the one who could
feel your heart beating
out of your chest
but maybe I made it all up
in my head

Was playing with me
the role of your lifetime?

A man of many faces
a boy still running races
to please everyone
but himself

Tried so hard to forget me
Even if I wasn't your one and only
I feel how much you regret me

Your love killed us slowly

I have a history of leaving
Just to keep my head above water

I've never been much into drowning
after all,
I am my mother's daughter

It's hard to get you off my mind
what brought you here this time?

I feel like a fool because of you
I got so swept up in
what we could have been
I never noticed the sharp edges
within you

And every time I would lean in
you took pieces of me with you

Never leaving me feeling fulfilled
just drained from the holes
you left in my soul

Even though
I know you tried so hard
to make all you lost
whole

Sometimes it slams into me
like a hurricane reaching for the shore

The waves of missing you
caught in the storm of wanting more

As much as I hope you feel my absence
As much as I wish I could make you feel

Every ounce of hurt and confusion
you left with me
when you said what we had
was never real

As much as I wish
for you to replay every kitchen dance
and touch of your hands on my skin

As much as I want these things
I know I shouldn't want

I still hope you know
I want what's best for you more

And if that's not me
I hope you find
whatever it is
you're looking for

And when the lights go down
do you think of the time
you wrapped your arms around
my waist
and pulled me close?

Do you think of my lips on your neck?
As she touches your chest?

Tell me, who do you see
when she is down on her knees?

I promised you
I'd be there in every whisper of her touch

It's hard to forget someone
who once gave you so much

In every bone of my body
I am tired of the wanting you
And the weights I place on my heart, ache
To keep from calling out your name

They say you cant find a lifeline
in someones uncertainty

But I kept holding onto nothing
in hopes that one day
you'd find me worthy

I knew this would be
how we'd end

You like to laugh
and play pretend
acting like you're innocent
telling everyone
your heart is on the mend

But it still belongs to her
and your false promises
I didn't catch them all at first

I got swept up in who you were
all the ways you made me feel alive

I thought you felt it too
but you had to run and hide

You will find in her absence
that she exists inside you
like a poison in your veins
the ghost of a girl
you wish had stayed

I hope you replay every time
you raised your voice at me,
every time you crossed a line

What my face looked like
is it etched in your mind?

Taking into account
all the things I can't live without

You're at the top of my list
of things I love to miss

Our expectations killed us
I quickly learned I would never be enough
to fill the hole In your chest
that was eating you up

There is no greater distance
than what lies between us at this table
I can recall every fight
and sleepless night
that led to what now ails us

Yet you carry yourself
like you can't feel us breaking

You stand up to leave
and still kiss me on the cheek

Do you even taste the tears that fell
as you lay next to me asleep?

It's hard to find the time
when the words we are dancing around

Are *goodbye*

Quiet bleeds into the morning
like the moment I let you go
it came without warning

A day when clouds lay heavy in the sky
like the earth is trying to match my mood
It too, holds back tears to cry

I've never had a problem being wanted
I've never had a problem capturing attention

The problems sneak in when they realize I'm a woman

With big dreams, needs, and wants

With big thoughts, feelings, and hopes

What's it take to find a heart who wants to hold mine?

Not just my body
but all of the things that keep me up at night

They all take small pieces of you, don't they?
The bodies that land in our beds

Another party.

Another blur.

Another warm body to take home at the end of the night.

It's not our fault really,
our generation has been conditioned to love like this.

Giving everything for the promise of nothing.

A solemn exchange of two lonely souls,
who couldn't take the loneliness any longer.

So, we'll have a drink for courage

and lose ourselves in a stranger's kiss.
If only just for a moment.

But as we lay here,
next to these bodies
of whatever their name is,
from whatever bar you stumbled out of together,
the ache in your chest grows.

Because their arms
do not stretch across the bed
as they feel you stir.

Their mouth does not rumple
into that maddening smirk.

The shade of their hair
is not the one you search for
in every crowd,
but you're far too gone
to feel anything now.

We say it's not our fault,
that we can quit if it ever feels right.
but what if it never does?

What if we give these pieces away,
so that eventually
when we look in the mirror

there won't be anyone there to blame

Do you avoid my street
like I do yours?

Do you take the new girls to
the places I showed you first?

10 years a veteran
in a town that sings you to sleep
with nothing to show for yourself
but a trail of broken lovers
and irredeemable dreams

No one ever talks much about the after
They tell me how strong I am for leaving
how much better off I'll be

What pride I must have for choosing myself
and all the ways it must feel
to finally be free

They'll never see the vices I bury myself under
or the ongoing waves of misery
or how I beg my mind to please stop questioning
all of the things
it seems to need

And even though I know this is what's best
I'm just a girl
with a heart that's been broken,
crushed
under the weight
of chosen grief

While they tell me it's not the end of a life
it's still the death of what could have been shared

The funeral of fantasized memories,
and the moments
he never found enough want to care

But this time I promised myself
I wouldn't let him sneak back in
on those fleeting moments of happiness
that always seemed to wear him much too thin

Later, I'd come to learn
that pain was all my heart had known
and all those feelings I found in him

I'd first felt at home

Didn't you see I was out of breath
but swimming to shore?
I guess we'll never know
who loved the other more

My best birthday present yet
was the gift of our quick death

Kind of cliche to end our
trip around the sun
over text

And I know I was losing my grip
but if you had only
laced your fingers in
I'm pretty sure
you'd still be tracing hearts
on my palm
with your fingertips

All the hoops jumped through
to be noticed by you,
and for what?

Only to change your mind
every 3 months

Do you miss me yet?
When you lay down at night,
do your dreams speak any regrets?

Please Go
Love her
Miss her
Grieve her

While I
Let go
Love often
Live for my lost time

And maybe

When we're all healed up
my heart will be right where you left it

In the split where the night
met a sun-soaked sky

A tightrope of indecision
lost in the potential of you and I

I miss and love you
every second of the day

Do you hide your face out of shame?

Aren't you curious
about what's happened
since you've been away?

If you were to take the time
and say a proper goodbye
by looking in my eyes

You would have seen
the greatest love die
all the hope I held onto
I just wanted to be in your life

In another life
I watch the sunrise warm your cheek
I watch your lips smirk
and your arms stir
as you reach for me

In another life there was no distance
we knew it was love in an instant

Do you see yourself?
All twisted in my words?
All I felt for you,
needed somewhere to go.

So, I'll put them in these pages
and let time pass me by.
In hopes that space will ease
the heartache of you and I.

The moon was pink last night
but I could only think of blue.
The same hue as yours -
god, I hope you miss me too.

When I fell for you it wasn't cliche

I fell for the way you show up for those you love
each and every day

I fell for the way your eyes crinkle
when your head falls back in a laugh

If I was ever too quiet
it's because getting lost in you
took the words right out of my mouth

I was afraid to let you see
the raging wars inside of me

And when I felt my depths scare you
I felt you pull away

I broke
when I finally understood
you would never love me that way

You say this wasn't your intention
Pray tell, what did you intend then?

With your nose nuzzled in my neck
your arms around my waist
getting lost in our musical haze
in rooms that were always
much too small to contain
all the ways we pretended
we weren't in pain

The night we met
you were wearing that mask
I swore you took it off
but I must've missed it
after one too many
sips from your flask

All the beautiful glimpses
you gave of your heart
were enough to keep me
stumbling toward you
in the dark
begging to find one piece
that fit just right
but then I realized
it was you
who kept turning out the lights

You can add this to your resume
as the role of your lifetime
while I float away, untethered
since you cut our lifeline

Maybe I feel so lost
because now I know
you were never honest

Do your eyes even tell you the truth
when they're staring back at you?

Late at night
in the crowded corners
of your room
where the "love of your life"
still waits to tuck you in

How can you idolize someone
who slept with your best friend?

I swear I'm not trying to judge
I swear I'm trying to understand
how all that happened in your life
turned you into this man

Please know, the only thing
I was hoping for
was the chance to hold your hand

Through the good and bad
the happy and sad
I never told you this but
you were only the second person in the world
I'd ever fantasized about being a dad

What did you really think of me?
was I just a shiny new toy
to distract you from reality?
When you couldn't even find the time
to be a friend to me?

Please know,
I, too, never intended
to wind up here
begging on my knees
for just a scrap of your attention
to forget your
ill-fated "intentions"

Is this how I let you go?
In the middle of the afternoon at 3:04?
When the grey clouds lay heavy overhead

Should I pick up the phone to call you instead?

Confusion seeps out of my pores
As I replay our memories from the Friday before

Your silence is the loudest scream I've ever heard

It cracks away at my armor
It makes me question my self worth

And I promise

You'll look for me
in all of the arms you fall into
only to find
they'll never quite fit

THE NEXT CHAPTER

One day
my words will find their way
to your shelf
and you'll reach for me
on the nights
you can't reach for anyone else

It's strange
how much can change
with just a bit of time

The leaves
with the seasons

The tide
with each new cycle of the moon

and my heart
with the way
it once loved you

I hope you know
I learned to let you go
with every ounce of ink
left in this pen

Marked on pages
that's where our love now lay

Smeared between bindings
for another forlorn heart
to stumble upon one day

You deserve someone who wants to choose you.
To claim you.
To grow and heal with you.
You deserve quality time and surprises.
You deserve honesty and prioritization.
You deserve kindness and accountability.
You deserve hugs from behind
      and kisses on your neck.
You deserve these things
        because you can provide them too.
Your love is coming soon.

I wish you well
I wish you laughter
I wish you peace

Please excuse me while
I tend to my needs

For love can't grow
where the past still covers
my heart like weeds

The morning light touches
    the dried tears on my cheek
Remnants of wars raised in my dreams

A new day is born out of the dark
One more chance
    for this bruised and battered heart

Arms of opportunity wait by the window
Begging, pleading, for me to please

Let go

Your time will come
Until it does, take joy in the little moments
    that make up your day

Remember, that what is yours
    will never pass you by

I hope you choose to heal
    in those seconds that feel so
    incandescent

So you may rise to meet her willingly
    when your destiny comes

I hope you continue to choose yourself
    over shitty people

I hope you choose to love
    every chance you get

And when someone loves you back
I hope you're brave enough to let them in

I lost us but found myself
Turns out I wasn't made
To be another broken doll
On your shelf

I wonder how long it will take to find you?
The one my soul dreams about
The one I long to wrap my arms around

And hear the secrets you hold tight
To learn the things that haunt your nights
I yearn for the days
When I can kiss the fears from your mind
I can't wait to tell you my story
The things that molded me as a child

I hope to create a space of healing
And when I say I love you, I will mean it

I'll keep living and dreaming for now
And when I finally meet you
I'll be ready to make that vow

Please know, I'm prepared to wait a lifetime
To finally call you mine

I hear that in 7 years time
every part of my body will be new

It will hold beautiful secrets

And not one inch will have been
touched by you

Thank you

Your absence has made me laugh harder and longer with friends who love me exactly as I am

You made me appreciative of the kindness and soft-spoken words of new lovers at 2 am

Thank you, for making me grateful for

the kind peace only a certain type of loneliness can bring

You made me realize that the
bare minimum is not acceptable,
even on the days you could reach it

Most importantly, *thank you*
for *showing me what love was*

by showing me what love wasn't

Life is too short to hold back.

From your dreams, from the truth, from love.
It's too damn short.

There will be regrets in this life - that is certain.
But do not let it be from holding back pieces of yourself
in hopes to fulfill some narrative
that was written FOR you,
not BY you.

So live freely, love easily, and have the courage to believe
you deserve good things.

I pulled love from nothing
And learned to stitch where I bled
Placed my wounded heart on a shelf

And finally put my past to bed

The magic we created was real
and I hope
even if for the shortest of times
I made you feel
like you were worthy
of a love
that wanted to learn you

I will be someone's first choice someday
I will have pancakes in the morning
and dances around the kitchen
I will know what arms around my waist
and kisses on the back of my neck
as sip my coffee feels like

I will know what it takes to build true vulnerability and trust
One day, I will know what it feels like
to be someone's priority

I will know a kind love
I will know a patient love

I will know a love
I get to call home

Sometimes I look at the moon
and wonder where you are

What part of the sky can you see,
with each our own blanket of stars?

Have you found peace
where you once felt at war?

Looking back at us in this moment
it's clear neither of us knew
what life had in store

I've tried to hide my hopelessly romantic heart

I've played the chill girl
The girl who acted like she couldn't care less

I've been the roster girl
I've been the heartless girl

And in succeeding at these roles,
I've gotten good at hiding my heart

But I am a lover girl
I am a soft girl
I am a romantic girl

I will not apologize for falling fast
And I won't hide these pieces of my heart any longer

Life is too short not to love fully, every day, and with intention

You often told me I must be too broken

Like the cracks life had left on my soul
had left me tainted
a little too open

Years down the road I sit
while the morning sun caresses my face
free from the weight of your expectations
my heart no longer feels the need to chase

But then, after some time
what they all said would happen, happened
I woke to the sun peeking through my windows

The world was quiet
as I lay sprawled in my bed

I let my eyes slowly focus
on the shades of yellow
that made their way up my sheets
to warm my skin for the day ahead

I made a place where all my broken parts
finally felt at home
and the arms I longed to turn to
I'd found within my own

And from this I know, even after all I've seen,
that peace will always find its way
to fill the cracks within my heart
and all the moments in between

But it won't be found
in what we think will be our greatest treasures
I find that peace exists
in what we make of life's greatest failures

I hope every day I wake up
and I'm worried a little less
that I will backslide
Into my demons

my used to be mess

I will dance under stars and countless moons
I will drink away the memory of you
I will sail to places you've never seen
I will dive into foreign waters and wash myself clean
I will evolve into a woman your hands have never roamed

I will return to myself

My fortress
My home

Dear reader,

If you find yourself lost in these pages, I'm sorry your heart is hurting. I hope it eases soon.

And if you relate to these words, be sure to follow me on socials @CarolineComposed, for updates on my next book **Good Girl; Good Luck,** and join me on my healing journey!

I'd love to walk alongside you.

All my love,
Caroline

Made in the USA
Columbia, SC
27 August 2024